In the Cards

A Collection of Memories Inspired by Lotería

Christina Saballos

Copyright © 2017 by Christina Saballos. 760040

Cover and interior photos by Edith Alvarez
ISBN: Softcover   978-1-5434-3083-7
       EBook   978-1-5434-3082-0

All rights reserved. No part of this book may be reproduced or transmitted in any form or by any means, electronic or mechanical, including photocopying, recording, or by any information storage and retrieval system, without permission in writing from the copyright owner.

Print information available on the last page

Rev. date: 07/15/2017

To order additional copies of this book, contact:
Xlibris
1-888-795-4274
www.Xlibris.com
Orders@Xlibris.com

In the Cards

A Collection of Memories Inspired by Lotería

— Christina Saballos —

Dedicated to:

Mom, my support

Ricky, my encouragement

Beni & Santi, my inspiration

Las Jaras – The Arrows

    Do you enjoy a good ghost story? The mystery and wonder of the circumstances. The goosebump-inducing details. Maybe you're a believer who has had an experience of your own - or waiting for that day. Have you considered the underlying sadness that often accompanies these tales of the unexplained? Some believe grief over the loss of a loved one, like an arrow piercing your heart, creates a longing so intense that you call the spirit world to you. Who wouldn't want to see that person once more, feel their presence beside them once more, or willingly go against all rational understanding just to heal the wound for that brief moment? And yet, here is a story about a spirit who doesn't let go. Doesn't it make sense that they grieve, too?

*****

    A pearl-colored glow dripped from the crescent that hung high against the black felt sky and seeped through the open window of the unlit bedroom. It wasn't a noise or even one of those sudden jerks of the leg that yanked Isidaro from his pillow, or rather, a rolled up pair of pants. The light must have done it. The light, blinding and somehow deafening at once. And now, across the room, Miguel lay frozen in his makeshift bed, frantically blinking sleep away for a clear view. It had to be a dream. Or the moonlight playing tricks on their blood-shot eyes. The last few days had been terribly exhausting. Aching grief and worry had reached unexpected heights at the funeral, less than eight hours ago. Yet, here she stood before them, the two brothers would swear upon her blessed soul the next morning.

Their sister, Emilia Llamas Macias, was a strong woman, orphaned at age ten and shuffled around until she was of an age to fend for herself. She married a musician, gave birth to two children who were six years apart, then was left by the musician to raise their children alone. Everyone called Emilia's daughter Pachita. The younger boy, born in 1903, was named Salvador. Years passed and Emilia enforced her strong Catholic views on the siblings. Pachita married, but Salvador grew into his twenties still without a wife or family of his own. He had moved from Guadalajara to Los Angeles when he was about sixteen years old and by 1929 he was a successful tailor with two or three employees of his own. That was the year the stock market crashed. That was also the year Emilia was diagnosed with cancer. She died in 1930. Salvador was twenty-seven years old, and he was devastated. Family members worried and wondered about him – how would he handle the loss especially because he was a single man without a wife to care for him? On the night of the funeral, Emilia's brothers, Isidaro and Miguel, insisted on staying with Salvador. And what they saw that night, no one spoke about until the next morning.

She appeared before them, dressed in the same cream-colored lace in which she was buried. A blurred, over-exposed photo version of their sister appeared out of the moonlight and floated through the sparse room, past the brothers, straight toward her sleeping son. She hovered over Salvador's bed, creating a veil of light around him, then slowly bent down to gently kiss his forehead. He never budged. And he didn't hear a word about it until the next morning when his uncles assured him that he would never be alone.

El Músico – The Musician

    Emilia Medina enjoyed the lively play and laughter of her children as they walked home from the small theatre. As a single mother in the early years of Jalisco's twentieth century, she did not have many opportunities to take pleasure in her children's amusement, let alone something as frivolous as a live stage production. The audience had dispersed quickly, leaving only the children, Emilia, and looming darkness on the long stretch of road. Amidst her daughter's delighted high-pitched squeals, she thought she heard a man's heavy footsteps behind her. Three times she looked back sure to find someone following her, but saw no sign of another person nearby.

    At home she put the children to bed and made herself comfortable for the night. Sleep was difficult to come by ever since her husband, Amado, had left them without much regard or resources. He had lost two of his fingers in an accident that involved firecrackers and it left him incapable of playing professional guitar - the only legal way he knew to earn a living. The last news Emilia had heard of him was that he had moved to California and had started a new family.

Abruptly, as if out of a dream, Emilia opened her eyes startled by the familiar sound of melodic strings. It was a sound she had not heard in two years, but recognized instantly. She looked in on the children who were still sleeping like bronze statues, immobile and perfect. She remembered how Amado used to play little tunes that either kept them entertained for hours or put them peacefully to sleep. Now, as the memory faded, she could no longer hear the music.

Returning to bed, she sank underneath the thick blankets, concluding that the music must have come from a neighboring home. Allowing the warmth and comfort to soothe her quickened heartbeat, she relaxed her tightened joints and muscles until sleep coyly tip-toed toward her.

* * * * *

It was too dark to distinguish objects in the room but in a moment of sudden recognition she knew a strong, calloused hand had gripped her right arm. Numb with fear, she heard a gruff whisper call her name, "Emil-i-a." In seconds, she was free from her bed, standing alert and defensive at her bedroom doorway. There was still a cloak of darkness in front of her but, somehow, she knew whatever she had felt and heard had gone. Stooped over the nightstand, she clumsily lit a candle and caught sight of something sticking out from under her pillow. A small, coarse piece of paper, with no message or label, was wrapped around a rolled up bundle of money. Emilia pieced apart the variety of muck-covered bills that smelled of damp earth and only then did she notice her right forearm, still sore where three thick fingerprints lay.

El Cantarito – The Water Pitcher

Salvador Medina and Elena Tapia married in May 1938. It was a jubilant celebration overflowing with family, friends and best wishes. No one wanted to miss the festivities (even if it meant riding in on a horse for three days) including Elena's closest cousin, Alberto. He was a few years older than she but they had grown up together, played together, and often confided in each other. Salvador enjoyed Alberto's company very much and understood that the cousins' relationship was more like brother and sister.

Soon after the wedding, Salvador and Elena moved into their first house together. It was an old-fashioned style structure with a kitchen open to the outside like a patio. There was a roof to keep the rain out, and a ledge to store supplies. Often, though, stray cats would sneak onto the ledge and fall asleep there. Elena diligently attempted to load the ledge with pots, pans, or anything else that would take up space. They enjoyed the house and those early years spent together. For some time nothing out of the ordinary haunted the newlyweds' routine.

In August of 1940, while the couple prepared for a family fiesta, which was to be held in two days, Alberto came to visit. Stepping inside the kitchen, Alberto found Elena on her tip-toes struggling to push a heavy ceramic water pitcher on to the ledge. He quickly clutched the pitcher and eased it into place.

"Prima, let me help you with that before you hurt yourself."

"Ay, thank you, Alberto."

When he turned to face her, she could see immediately that something was wrong.

"Alberto, what's wrong? You look terrible, like you haven't slept in days."

"I'm in trouble," he blurted out. "I met a girl. We're in love."

Elena chuckled. "Well, that's good news -"

"She's fifteen, prima...and pregnant."

The two cousins sat at the table, Elena listened intently to Alberto's story. He was 27 years old and his pregnant unwed love just a girl. Her father, Senor Ibarra, was a hateful drunk who would rather see his daughter's reputation tainted than allow her to marry Alberto. He despised Alberto for reasons only he knew and had forbidden his daughter to see him.

By the time Alberto left Salvador and Elena's house, he had decided to plead to the girl's father - talk man to man. He would go to their home the next day and then update his cousin with the outcome as soon as he could. Throughout the next day Elena thought of Alberto's predicament and at night, while she lay in bed, she said a special prayer - that her cousin would find peace and happiness. That time of year was what the people called Tiempo de Aguas, when the rain came down incessantly. Was it the pounding drops against the roof that were keeping her up or the weight of her worry for Alberto?

In the black of night, a thunderous crash pierced Elena's quiet sleep. She shot right out of bed, stunned that Salvador had not stirred, but certain that a cat had knocked over the ceramic pitcher while taking refuge from the rain. Prepared to find broken pieces scattered on the cement floor, she was met instead by a kitchen in perfect order. The pitcher sat where Alberto had placed it. There were no cats anywhere. After she searched the house a bit more and found nothing out of place, she shrugged the incident off and returned to bed. It was around eleven o'clock.

The following morning Salvador and Elena rose to prepare for the fiesta planned for that evening. They received a knock on the door. Hoping it might be Alberto with some news, Elena opened the door but instead saw her mother, Conchita, with a grave look on her face.

"Mamá, what is it?"

"What? Nothing. I'm just tired."

Elena, noticing her mother's trembling hands, persisted.

"Something's wrong. Tell me."

"It's Alberto. He...he is in the hospital. He had an accident. But...there's nothing we can do now. People will be arriving soon. Is the food ready?"

"Mamá, wait. Stop!" Elena yelled. "Is Alberto alright? Is it serious? We should go see him."

Conchita paced, wringing her hands until they were red. "No, no, no. He's not in the hospital. He's dead. I didn't know how to tell you. He's dead."

There were not many known details. All Conchita had heard was that authorities had found Alberto's body stabbed at the house of Senor Ibarra sometime around eleven o'clock the night before.

El Cazo – The Saucepan

In January of 1947, Salvador and Elena moved into a house in the city of Moorpark. Located in Ventura County, 50 miles northwest of Downtown Los Angeles, Moorpark was rumored to be named after a type of apricot. Many fertile fields and crops, primarily apricots, populated the budding community; and with them were hardworking families making an honest living off of the land. The couple moved into the beautiful ranch-style structure with their three children, and thought they had hit the jackpot. An expansive lawn, wide porches all around the outside walls, and sunlit views of fields surrounded by rolling hills - an exterior that offered luminous rays of hope and lush promises.

Inside, the house was a tomb. The front door opened into a main (once-living) space covered in dreary layers of dust, stagnant air, and rat droppings. Yes, the rats surely made their home in the nooks and crannies oof torn upholstery and occupied cabinets and shelves. The couple was surprised to find the house fully furnished albeit with outdated items. Knick-knacks still sat out in the open while cans and jars remained in the kitchen.

"Whoever lived here left in a hurry," commented Salvador.

"Well, it's ours now," replied Elena.

The couple, and their three children set to work and thoroughly cleaned the rat-infested house that appeared to have been abandoned for some time (there exist even first-hand accounts of the mild-mannered Salvador incorrigibly swinging a dead rat in the faces of his misbehaving kids). It didn't take long for the family to wipe the past clean, comfortably settle in with their own things, then uncover far more profound stains.

There were numerous minor incidents where strange noises were heard or odd images appeared but no one paid much attention to them. Salvador thought he heard a voice crying out from the bathroom while he served himself a plate in the kitchen. Wondering why nobody had yet attended to whoever was in the bathroom, he passed the dining table where Elena and all three kids sat eating dinner together. Elena noted his confusion.

"What's wrong with you?"

"Is someone in the bathroom?"

"No. We're all right here. Why? What is it?"

"No, nothing" he said, shaking it off.

On another day, Elena's brother tried repeatedly to convince the family that he saw a woman he'd never seen before standing in the garage beckoning him to go to her. But, the heat had reached 90 degrees, and he was drunk so the others teased him that it was probably wishful thinking.

Eventually, Elena and Salvador fell onto hard times. They had to sell their car, and they lost the house. On one of the last days they were to remain in the house, Elena prepared a large saucepan for her family's favorite meal, chicken *mole*. Salvador was outside in the nearby peanut fields, and the kids were coming in and out with baskets from the fields. With her concentration on the sizzling and bubbling stove and her back facing the rest of the kitchen, Elena suddenly felt that she was not alone. Knowing for a fact that each of her kids had left the house for another round of pickings, she couldn't shake the sensation that someone else was in the room (You've felt it - that shift in molecules or slight change of air that spurs goosebumps on the arm or stifles your breath). Determined not to carry on with such childishness, she stirred the contents of her saucepan until she heard a heavy sigh, like that of a tired woman coming in from the heat.

"Socorro, is that you?"

Hoping to see her eldest daughter, she turned but didn't see anyone. The house was silent and empty. She continued cooking until she heard an even louder sigh, this time closer than before. She froze when her vision fell on the shiny metal reflection on the saucepan and in it saw a matronly figure, gasping for air, hover directly behind her. Before she was completely crippled by fear, Elena dashed out of the house and cut across her neighbor's yards until she reached the peanut fields, wooden spoon still in hand.

One of the neighbors, Lucita, had become a good friend to Elena. After they had moved out of the beautiful ranch-style, Lucita told Elena a very interesting story. Lucita's aunt was the woman who had lived in the house before Elena and her family moved in. The woman had allowed her niece and her husband to move in with her. The husband was no good. Trouble from the start. He was caught up in all sorts of schemes and should never have been trusted. One day he tried to rob the woman, but the situation escalated until he choked her to death, her last breath stifled on her own kitchen floor. He ran away, and no one heard from him again. Lucita and her children moved into a house nearby. It wasn't much later that Elena and Salvador arrived and took the house as their own - but, of course, it never really was.

La Muerte – The Death

Many stories about my grandparents impress me with their examples of strength and fortitude, but there is one in particular that literally clenches my heart and doesn't let go until I can find proper distraction.

Every time I try to write it, I feel I don't do it justice so I'll share it here the only way I know how - the way it was told to me.

In July of 1950, my grandmother, Elena, was traveling by train from Mexicali to Guadalajara. A very popular 48-hour trip at that time as I understand it. While my grandfather stayed in Los Angeles to work, she planned to visit her family and had by her side her five children (Socorro, Salvador Jr., Mary, George, and Alfredo) ranging in ages from 10 years to 5 months. It was nearly impossible to keep 4 children behaved and entertained while looking after an infant, then add to that, the summer heat which provoked irritability more than a sense of adventure.

Well into the first night, Elena's youngest, Alfredo, developed a high fever. By the second night, his fever had gone beyond 104 degrees. While struggling to bring her boy's temperature down, Elena begged for help from people on the train. All they could do was recommend that she get off at the next stop and find a doctor. She did just that. A sympathetic lady who had been on the train offered to look after the other four kids at her home while Elena rushed to the hospital. Faced with limited options, she trusted the lady with her children. According to the four kids (my aunts and uncles), this lady and her husband were God-sends in a dire situation. They were fed well and provided with comfortable beds. Back at the hospital, Alfredo was reportedly so hot with fever that his skin crackled at the touch and blood ran from his small nose. He died there.

No one remembers the name of the town, but it was what one would call a poor shanty town, full of boxcars that people made into their homes. On July 17th, Alfredo was buried without a gravestone in the nameless town. No one else in our family ever visited the gravesite and I'm not sure anyone knows where to go if they wanted to. Perhaps because Alfredo was only 5 months old, but no pictures of him were ever taken. Hardly any proof of him at all.

Elena boarded the train a second time back to Los Angeles with her four children and a pair of Alfredo's shoes.

On July 17, 1951, exactly one year after his burial, my mother was born. She was named Sylvia Consuelo - *consuelo*, which means to comfort in a time of grief.

El Violoncello – The Cello

 Sylvia heard the deep, warm tones of the cello coming from the dining room and quickly turned off her small transistor radio. Not much could tear her away from the seductive rhythms of Mary Wells, Marvin Gaye, The Supremes or her favorite, Smoky. But when her older brother practiced the cello, she was transported to distant places that looked nothing like the confined, chipped-painted walls of their home. She didn't know much about classical instruments or any music besides motown and her parents *rancheras*, but for some reason, those low melodic notes made her think of places she saw only on television. She imagined great concert halls bigger than her school auditorium even where fancy ladies in the audience sparkled with jewels and the musicians wore black suits with those wide belt-things around their waists.

 Her brother, Sal, played on, oblivious to the world around him. She was careful not to let him see her. In the last few months, he had grown more irritable, snapping insults at anyone who interrupted his concentration. Crouched against her mother's heavy china cabinet, she watched the back of Sal's head, gently tilted toward the fingerboard, and tried to picture him on the stage of one of those great concert halls. She didn't know where he'd get a nice suit, but she was sure he would look quite handsome in one. The whole family could make a special trip to see him play. They might be asked to sit in the very first row because they were related to him. She could ask her older sister, Mary, to sew a new dress for her - maybe borrow one of her pill-box hats!

The music stopped. Jolted out of her daydream, Sylvia heard the rustling of sheet music and watched Sal readjust himself in his seat. Facing the sun-drenched window, he sat upright and began a piece she recognized as one of Johann Sebastian Bach's creations. Sal played it more than any other. It was her favorite. Sylvia soaked in the melancholy melody and forgot all about the lingering smell of two-day old beans abandoned on the stove and the chill of the hardwood floor underneath her bare legs. Instead, she lost herself beyond the dining room window. Sal's somber notes seemed to serenade the gray clouds as they lumbered past the sun. A blanketing feeling of love and sorrow wrapped around her. Love for her mysterious older brother who made such beautiful music. Sadness that she could not explain.

There was no way she could know. It was too early to foresee. It would be at least another year before he'd see a doctor. Two more years before he'd be properly diagnosed. She would bear witness to his paranoid fits, hallucinations, and disorganized thoughts. She would visit him in eerie institutions and hear bizarre accounts of electro-shock therapy. She would routinely rescue him from the streets when he'd wander aimlessly. She would hurry in the night to be by his side when he would pass in his sleep. And she would always escape to better places when remembering the transportive magic of his cello.

La Botella – The Bottle

    The occasional drive to my mom's childhood home in the El Sereno hills was always a special treat. These jagged hills did not proudly display grand edifices purchased at high prices for their luxurious picture-window views. Recklessly strewn together, the homes in the neighborhood instead held quick-tempered young citizens who were born into near-poverty and resided somewhere between American and *Mexicano*.

    After breakfast at Nena's Mexican Restaurant, I would beg my parents for the short detour that took us through narrow spiral roads and the retelling of countless adventures featuring hooligan rebellion. With eleven children and two adults packed into one small house, it is no surprise that the living energy behind its walls would push forth and conquer the surrounding hills. There was no shortage of stories my mom could tell. Each driving tour ignited a new memory.

Here is one of my favorites…

    In 1976, my mom was 24 years old with 8 and 9 year old sons. While she worked late shifts at the post office and my dad was still at the factory, the boys were left with her parents and younger siblings at the old house. There was a family with 2 teenage daughters who lived up the street – we'll call them the Lopez's (they costarred in a series of tales from the past). One of these Lopez daughters had a son who was also 9 years old and played often with my brothers. For whatever reason, a fight/argument/disagreement broke out between my older brother and the Lopez kid. His mother wasn't around, I suppose, so he took his case to his aunt who, by all trustworthy accounts, was certifiably insane. Since calm mediation is not usually a priority of the certifiably insane, she opted instead to launch an empty beer bottle at my brother's head. All hell broke loose.

The bottle had just grazed his right temple - didn't even require stitches. But it was enough to set off my mom's younger brothers – a rascally trio – who tried in vain to threaten the Lopez's with my mom's inevitable wrath.

"You better watch out."

"My sister don't take shit from nobody."

"Oh man, she's gonna beat your ass."

"What is your skinny sister going to do? We're not afraid of her," were reportedly the snide comments from Mama Lopez, who had graciously appeared as her daughter's spokesperson in the matter .

Before work the next day, my mom dropped the boys off at the old house as usual. With sponge curlers still in her hair, she snatched one of her brothers' belts (those 2 inch-thick ones made of real cowhide leather), marched halfway up the hill to the Lopez house, and hollered for that crazy bitch to come out. Man, what a scene it must have been! My mom yelling things like, "You belong in a mental hospital. They oughtta lock you up and throw away the key. Let me throw a bottle at you, see how you like it" while flanked by her younger instigating brothers. Her mother, my grandma, pleaded with her to stop before the cops showed up, while her aunt encouraged her to "defend your child like any good mother would". That 17-year-old bottle-thrower had the nerve to meet my mom on the street, but before she got a word or anything else in, she was wrestled to the ground by 100-pounds of maternal rage, flipped onto her stomach, and mercilessly whipped in front of the crowd like bad-behaved girls ought to be. At least, that's how my mom tells it.

While I'm usually labeled the spitting-image of my mom, I don't lean towards her fiery temper and brazen kick-ass mentality. I can only hope that once my baby arrives, Mom's *badassness* tucked somewhere deep inside me will wake from its slumber and wreak havoc on any bottle throwers who take aim at my kid.

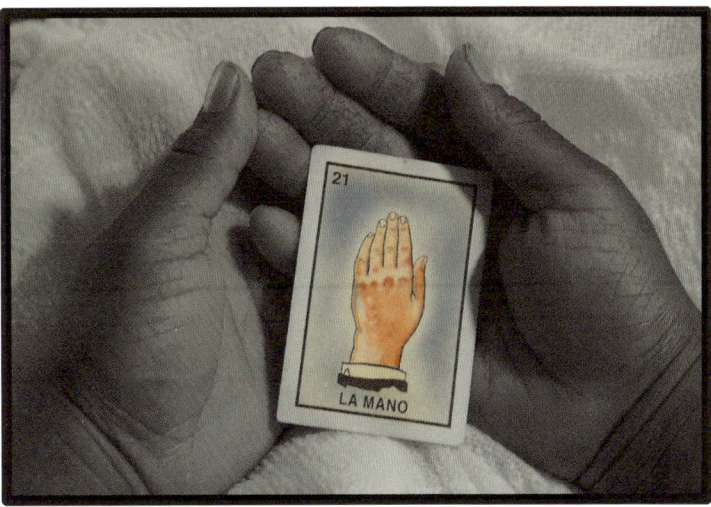

La Mano – The Hand

The gush of blood surprised him. It came as quickly and unexpectedly as had the rage. Eight seconds after the last blow, hand sent message to head that it was in pain. Nothing too bad - he had felt it a dozen times before. Deliberately, he released the tension in his right hand, regarding the white knuckles. His fist must have been tightly clenched because its color was just now returning. He considered the speed of his reflexes and began to feel grateful. His mind thought something, and without having to be asked twice, his hand had reacted. No explanation necessary.

At 16 years old he was sick of explanations. Mom. Counselors. Judge. Girlfriend. They always wanted answers, justifications, tell me one good reason why I should. Like when Mom set her fists atop her thick hips as she waited for him to explain why he needed twenty dollars. Because he wanted to take Gina to the movies, so they could be normal teenagers, so he could feel her soft fingers entwined with his, so he could erase the memory of cold handcuffs wrapped around his wrists. But Mom said she didn't have twenty dollars. Figured. They'd have to hang out here tonight.

When nothing else went is way, at least he knew he could count on his dependable hands. His Mom used to tell him and his brothers that if they refused to go to school they'd be forced to work with their hands for the rest of their lives. What was so wrong with that? None of them bothered with school. His father had refused to work with his hands or anything else, and four children were not enough to convince him otherwise. Good. He didn't need him anyway. If he saw his father on the street, he probably wouldn't recognize him, and if he did, he'd give him a right jab to the nose.

He stared at both palms, his squat fingers spread apart, and made a promise to his future. He would never leave his family. He loved Gina. She had a perfect smile that stretched all the way up to her eyes. All you could see was a twinkle. He could definitely see himself marrying her someday. He would work hard for his wife. He would depend on his hands because he could count on them – they listened – they were reliable. His right hand had come to his aid a whole bunch of times and the mess it left behind was usually satisfying, if not downright rewarding to see. But now, pulling his gaze away from his hands, he felt his stomach rise....

On his beat up mattress, she stirred. He would have rushed to her, held her, told her what a shit he was, but the blood stopped him. The flood of crimson, like cheap wine he often stole from the liquor store, didn't look right against her delicate features and white teeth that were now clenched in agony. Her nose was an uprooted bridge that haphazardly stood between the forehead and two streams that bled into one. He would have loved to have looked into her gray eyes and prove his sincerity when he begged forgiveness, but he couldn't. One gray eye was buried deep inside a swollen blue-black lump.

What had she done? What had set him off? He couldn't even remember, but he knew instantly he had been betrayed. He brought his hand away from his mouth where it was stifling an all-too-eager cry. Gina! He glared at it, realizing he could never trust it again.

La Sirena – The Siren

Dedicated to those women I grew up watching, not on television but in real life.

*****

    When I was a little girl, I thought my female teenage cousins were the shit! We came from a large family with many aunts, uncles, and kids, but there was a recognizable divide between those considered children - around 12 years old and under - and those who most certainly were not ever to be mistaken or mis-categorized as children – 15 years old and up.

    At family parties, these 4 or 5 young women would gather in a bedroom covered wall-to-wall with

Prince or Pat Benatar posters, blast extremely loud American Bandstand favorites, and plot the newest yet not terribly inventive way they were going to dupe their parents this weekend. Naturally, us younger kids weren't allowed in that bedroom for more time than it takes to yell "food's ready", but in that instant, you could pick up a strong collective whiff of freshly-popped Bubble Yum, plastic jelly-bean sandals, and Aqua Net...a lot of Aqua Net.

The hair was an art form. It defied gravity. I don't know what was going on in the Big-Hair state of Texas, but what these girls were doing could certainly rival it and any impenetrable bird's nest. From what I could gather, a few vital steps were necessary to achieve this look.

1. Blow dry wet hair.
2. Tease, tease, tease. Leave no hair unteased.
3. Use comb and fingers to shape.
4. Hairspray until it's no longer safe to secretly light a cigarette in your room.

One last thing to remember, your hair should be proportionately larger than your fluorescent hoop earrings. And the bigger the hoops, the better.

There's a picture of two of my cousins, Alice & Valerie, wearing off-the-shoulder polka dot blouses, plastic turquoise beads dangling around their necks, and bright pink plastic Ray-Bans. They're both puckering their lips seductively to the camera. Man, that's cool! I remember thinking to myself. They don't care what anybody thinks. I wish I was just like them. One boring day, some of my cousins thought it would be fun to play Photo Shoot - one of the few make-believe games they weren't too cool for - where we all throw tons of makeup on, dress crazy, and take pictures like supermodels. They did our makeup for us, the little girls, then got decked out in my aunt's halter dresses and heels. We looked like little posed dolls with baby fat and tangled hair. They were beautiful. Sparkling brown eyes, tan skin, petite bodies, and natural charm for days. Beautiful.

No wonder so many boys came around when the cousins showed up. One guy cried right there in front of everybody when Alice broke up with him. We all felt embarrassed for him. Alice closed the front door on him to prep for her date. My mom and I ran into this other guy at the video store who saw our last name and asked if we knew Angie. We said we did, as a matter of fact, and he told us that he had the biggest crush on her, but every day she thought up new reasons not to talk to him in class. He had to give her credit for the time she sat with cotton balls in her ears while her friend explained to him that Stephanie had an ear infection and couldn't hear anything. But I can't talk about unsuspecting lovesick boys lured in by enchanting females without mentioning Raquel. She signed her name Rock-el in all the yearbooks when she graduated high school. Led Zeppelin, Van Halen, and Blondie were her favorites. She showed up to our family reunion in the park wearing skin-tight black jeans zipped up the back, fitted red and black Rolling Stones t-shirt cropped at the waist with the sleeves cut off, and her jet-black hair feathered out to perfection. Not the most appropriate setting for blood-red lipstick and half a tube of eyeliner, but she knew how to pull it off. Minutes after her arrival, the reunion was notably larger than ever before with unfamiliar mustached faces circling her table.

Screw the Madonnas and Susana Hoffs, the Christie Brinkleys and Cindy Crawfords, the Demi Moores and Molly Ringwalds! My idols weren't on posters or the silver screen. They were live and in person, and my family.

Now let's take a moment of silence for those poor souls who pursued the siren's song, only to be crushed against the rocks.

El Sol – The Sun

    His first murder was in the summer of 1984. From March through June of the following year, he killed ten people in the cities of Rosemead, Monterey Park, Monrovia, Burbank and Pico Rivera. I lived in East L.A, a nearby city. A very nearby city.

    1985 was Los Angeles' hottest summer in 100 years. Thick, wool-blanket-heat covered the city and suffocated in its inhabitants the slightest hint of motivation. I was 7 years old. My cousins Lorrie and Arlene were 7 and 9 respectively. My childhood summers cannot be recalled without them. Each of us was the youngest sibling, drawn to each other by the same sense of mischief and curiosity. Neither of us big fans of dolls or mini plastic baking ovens, we watched movies like The Goonies and Monster Squad while imagining ourselves as those brave, adventure-seeking youngsters. We spent most of our days in and around

Arlene's house - a white single-story, three-bedroom in San Gabriel with a detached garage and an overgrown backyard -a deserted battlefield of scattered plastic lounge chairs and deflated balls. Beyond the back fence was an undeveloped half acre piece of land we were not to enter under any circumstances.

July 2nd, 1985 was reported as the hottest day in 100 years. He killed three more people that day. On July 7th, two women were murdered in Monterey Park and the press declared a serial killer was loose in Los Angeles County. They dubbed him The Nightstalker.

I hadn't had much experience with death. I think it's safe to say my cousins hadn't either. Our Grandpa had passed away the previous year leaving our parents, aunts, and uncles with a sorrow still deep and freshly planted inside each of them. Sure, us kids missed the gentle old man who comforted us on his lap, but what did we truly know of death and loss? We carried on through the heat as we always had - draped around the television watching music videos and Grease until we knew all the words, with afternoon strolls to the corner store for Fritos and Orange Crush, occasional splashes in the plastic drug-store pool laid out on the grass, and backyard rummages.

It was customary, if not crucial, to leave windows open all night long during the stifling summer. Our homes didn't have central air. Maybe a bedroom or living room had a clunky air-conditioner jammed into a window, but many folks sat outside on their porches or under umbrellas until bedtime where they then lay flat and uncovered ready to welcome the slightest breeze.

The Nightstalker liked open windows. Detectives found no forced entry in most of the homes he hit, but always an open or unlocked window. On July 20th, he struck at a home in Glendale. The next morning headlines read "Nightstalker Strikes Again" and "LA Bolts Its Doors, Windows." The city was hysterical. Locksmiths were busy around the clock. Security devices increased in sales. Guns and attack dogs were in high demand but could not be supplied fast enough. Someone reported that the Nightstalker preferred white and beige-colored houses; a mere coincidence that led to freshly painted houses across L.A.'s neighborhoods. And in these neighborhoods, volunteer watch groups formed to keep an eye on the streets through those long nights.

Sitting around the television at Arlene's house one day, our moms and dads and big brothers and sisters watched news reports about the serial killer. We overheard bits and pieces of information detailing horrific cases of murder and rape: on the wall he drew a pentagram out of blood, he was a devil worshiper, he hovered over the victim with a machete, that last murder happened just a block away from so-and-so's house. My Uncle Bill, who lived in Alhambra, swore to God that The Nightstalker was at his house but he had "scared that motherfucker away." To us kids, it seemed like the movies were coming to life. Our parents had been lying to us when they said Michael Myers, Jason Voorhees, and Freddie Krueger weren't real. Not only were they real, but our parents were terrified of them, too.

Another set of murders in Diamond Bar on August 8th, and the next few weeks continued without a sign of The Nightstalker. It would be unfolded later that he had traveled to San Francisco and killed another couple in the Lakeside District near Lake Merced. While he was away, investigators finally pinpointed a suspect and released his name along with a mugshot photo. His face was plastered on every newspaper in southern California. And his name was Richard Ramirez.

On Saturday, August 31st, I was home with my parents and brothers on S.Vancouver Avenue. Breaking News interrupted the regular programming to report the capture of Richard Ramirez! After arriving at the East Los Angeles Greyhound bus station early that morning, he quickly realized that he had been identified and recognized by citizens at every corner. A chase, not by police officers but by neighborhood men, that took him on and off a local bus, through backyards and into a stolen car, finally ended on Hubbard Street where he was taken down and held until law enforcement arrived. Hubbard Street. Less than a ten-minute walk from my childhood home. A neighborhood with a bad reputation had come together to fight a common enemy, and they had won. There were parties in the streets that night!

The end of the hottest summer in 100 years coincided with the capture of a real-life monster. The fear dissipated. A new school year started. Life returned to normal. The heat….well, that never really went away.

El Melon – The Melon

    By 10am, the temperature had nearly reached 90 degrees. Arlene, Lorrie, and me - three cousins almost in our pre-teens, fended for ourselves upon waking that Monday morning. All of the adults were at work, and the designated babysitter was Arlene's teenage sister who scarcely removed herself from a rigorous all-day beauty regime. After bowls of fruit loops and two deafening hours of MTV, Lorrie's thick black bangs began to stick to her moist forehead and my eyes glazed over with suffocating boredom. Arlene took charge of the situation, as always, being two years older than me and Lorrie and hesitantly declared it was time to get in the pool.

    The pool, unlike the neighbor's, was a flimsy plastic contraption purchased from a drugstore and set on the front lawn because the backyard had no grass, only dirt. Dressed in brightly colored swimsuits that struggled across our baby fat, we emptied the pool of yesterday's mosquito bedazzled water and filled it anew. The chilly nips at our skin were refreshing for about ten minutes. The pool was by no means big enough for three girls to swim or even stretch out in. Having tried before, we usually ended with unintentional kicks in each other's faces. Steadily, an array of bugs showed up for a quick dip that inevitably resulted in accidental suicides. Arlene's family dog, named Lady, made her way over from some un-ladylike venture that left her blonde coat caked with dirt. An easy leap over the unstable rim and she was in the pool, spreading mud and the fragrance of hot, wet dog.

Not much later, the three of us sat atop the roof of the garage – a new vantage point we had recently discovered. In our now sun-drenched swim suits, we nibbled at carved slices of juicy cantaloupe and day-dreamed about the neighbor's built-in pool and its possibilities. Games of Marco-Polo and chicken-fights, swimming races Arlene would always win, and parties where you'd only leave the water to eat and hit the piñata. Hope quickly scized us like when we'd hear the musical promise of an ice-cream truck three blocks away because out came the little neighbor girl in her swim suit. We watched her jump in all by herself with no one to race or play with and thought what an opportune moment this was for everyone involved. Neighbor girl could get three new friends, and we in turn could get the pool! In her friendliest tone, Arlene asked if we could join her and then proceeded with an itemized list of benefits that included plenty of yummy cantaloupe to share, an extended knowledge of pool-games to be played by four people, and a never-before-released invitation to visit our clubhouse. No way could she turn it down. Neighbor-girl responded with a steadfast "NO" before strutting back inside and closing the door behind her.

It's difficult to describe what we felt at that very moment. Heartache and disappointment was unequal to any un-purchased but desired toy or gadget. A blazing heat, not caused by the sun, scorched a hole in our chests worse than any chest cold had ever caused and far beyond the healing powers of Vicks VapoRub. Not yet interested in boys, this was the most painful of rejections our young souls had experienced. And it would be our first lesson in adolescent retaliation, as we each willfully launched every last cantaloupe skin into the neighbor's swimming pool.

Time stood still. We stood still, atop the garage, staring at our work. The dozen or so crescent-moon shaped cantaloupe skins waded lazily in the otherwise pristine pool. The ruthless midday sun penetrated the heavily chlorinated water, inciting a lively concert of glistening and sparkle that only water and gemstones can orchestrate. Despite the intrusion of cantaloupe skins, the swimming pool flaunted its allure like an oasis in the desert, or to children specifically, like a rainbow-sprinkled-frosting-covered-cream-filled-something on any day of the week. If it wasn't for the shared feeling of accomplishment, we would have acknowledged our envy of those discarded, half-eaten fruit peelings.

La Campana – The Bell

RRRRIIIINNNNGGGG

The first school bell sliced through the chatter and thrill of the small yard on Amalia Street. Twenty pairs of black and white leather oxfords scurried past the sun-scarred swings and canopied lunch tables.
"Line up now. Everybody line up," a friendly-faced woman with blonde hair called out to the group.
Tiny bodies topped with French braids, pony tails, crew cuts, and parts perfectly combed by Mama for the first day of first grade in 1985. In the classroom we sat at our own desks in alphabetical order by our last names - Arevalo, Beltran, Delgado, Del Hoyo, Diaz…..

There were no desks back in kindergarten. Us kids sat on the carpeted floor most of the time. Here, I felt like a grown-up professional. I couldn't wait to get my hands on some paper and start writing something. The walls were covered with bright posters, charts, letters and numbers. In the front left corner of the room, facing us as we worked at our miniature desks, was a statue of the Virgin Mary and an open children's bible on a reading stand. On the right wall was a handmade chart with each of our names in block letters and a pocket made of construction paper under each name. The key above explained:

Yellow = 1st warning

Red = 2nd warning

Black = Final warning

Depending on the crime, Ms. Cortez would stick a bookmark-size slip of yellow, red or (Yikes!) black paper under our name. Surely, she spotted the bad boy from the get go with his mop of black hair and a toothy grin that screamed, "I'm trouble." He got a black slip on day one, and it never left.

RRRRIIIINNNNGGGG

Third grade marked our promotion from the Small Yard to the Big Yard. No sandbox or swings on the south side of the building. The fenced-in land of kickball, basketball, handball and the occasional game of Chinese jump-rope was selflessly guarded by the noble Spartan painted on the wall. Here, Third, Fourth, and Fifth graders were forced to intermingle during precious minutes of freedom.

A small-scale war on a cement battlefield every weekday. Teachers on duty risked their lives against torpedo balls- yellow, orange, and maroon- coming from every angle, clusters of children skipping, running, tumbling, leaping in a medley of activity spread out over half a block. Then, just as the energy reached its peak, (just when an adult's patience was sure to run out), the high-pitched squeals could get no louder, and bodily injury was milliseconds away -

RRRRIIIINNNNGGGG

Day one of the Fifth grade was a big deal for two reasons. First, our classroom was now on the second floor along with those of the Sixth, Seventh, and Eighth graders. No fraternization with the kiddies down below. We were all about the penthouse level with a flight of stairs outside that led directly to the second floor. Even our trips to the bathroom could result in big-kid interactions. Oh! And a sanitary napkin machine! Had no idea what was in there when I was ten. Gumballs? Packets of sugar? It didn't matter.

The second cause for excitement (and just a pinch of pre-teen arrogance) in the Fifth grade was the long-awaited skirt. We tossed aside our one-piece jumpers and with them our adolescence. If any one of us had understood the significance of burning bras, we would have torched the jumpers. And don't let yourself be seen with a skirt past your knee. Total square. All you had to do was roll it up from the waist and BOOM. You're two inches cooler. Rumor was a nun would make you get on your knees and if your skirt didn't touch the ground, you were in trouble. Nobody I knew had that happen to them. Man, we were Fifth graders! The elders of the Big Yard. Who's gonna give us static?

BONG...BONG...BONG....

The church bell at St. Alphonsus rang through the streets, from Beverly to Whittier Boulevard, announcing the start of mass and the Eighth graders' eagerly anticipated commencement ceremony. Some

of us had been there since that first day of First grade. Others came along later. But, once you were in, you belonged to the class, and every moment from then on was a shared experience with the same two dozen little brothers and sisters in faith. Through potty accidents, bloody noses, and puberty. With good teachers, bad teachers, and nuns who pinched to quiet us down because they cared. Out of the scandals that rocked the playgrounds - She said she's not my friend anymore! Did you hear they kissed behind the stage? Alongside the burgeoning rebels, jocks, honor roll geeks, divas, and wallflowers. We were in it together.
"Line up now. Everybody line up," Ms. Kirby directed.

Girls and boys paired up by height in a slow choreographed procession of royal and sky blue caps and gowns, like a soft ocean wave flowing down the middle aisle toward the altar. Toward their futures.

La Palma – The Palm

 It was the summer of 1974 when the young Palm was first brought to the house on Vancouver Avenue. The local gardener, Ignacio (who liked to be called Nacho) selected this particular palm for the new family who had recently purchased the home and who had requested that a tree be planted in front of the house. He agreed that it was a good idea to provide some shade and add a little something to the bare yard.

 "I'll bring it tomorrow." he told the baby-faced man of the house as they discussed his vision for his new yard.

 Nacho drove leisurely through the wide neighborhood streets he knew better than his own aging body these days. In the back of the old patchwork yellow pick-up, the Palm fanned its sprightly leaves through the warm breeze passing overhead. The ladder, coiled waterhose, mower, and rake all held on tight, not participating in the Palm's excitement. They knew they were only along for the ride - just another gig for the seventh day in a row. They'd be spending another night in Nacho's garage that felt like the inside of an empty tin can. But not the little Palm.

They quietly wondered, what must it feel like to rest in a bed of earth under a blanket of night sky?

Nacho had just finished gently patting down the dirt around the Palm's base when the family arrived, pulling their cotton-candy-blue Chevy Malibu into the long strip of driveway. From its new residence in the ground - the front right corner of the square lawn - it had an advantageous view of all the comings and goings related to the house. With its outstretched leaves atop the long narrow stem, it stood silent, tall, and proud like a Buckingham Palace Foot Guard. The mother and father were youthful, vibrant people - opening and closing doors, grabbing bags, directing the little ones all in one spontaneous kaleidoscope of motion and color. And the little ones- two boys, six and seven years old in mirror-image maroon corduroy and striped t-shirt ensembles. Coyly, the Palm waved a hello, and the boys took it as an invitation to feel and poke with inherent curiosity until they were sufficiently appeased by its presence. Seconds later the boys could be heard enticing their pet German Shephard, and the Palm was left alone to breathe in all the comforts of its new home.

By the time August made way for September, the watchful Palm had learned a few indelible truths of the street. First, the old Japanese lady next door with the sharp eyes and sharper nose liked to peek through her curtains to make sure the boys did not set feet on her freshly-trimmed grass. The loyal Palm would try to warn them, but they never listened. Their mother told the crabby old lady on more than one occasion to "go find a hobby." Second, there seemed to be a surplus of stray dogs in the neighborhood. From itty-bitty trembling ones to gray and gruff monsters - all of whom would have raised a leg to the timid Palm had it not been for the man of the house shooing them away. It was a not-so-well-kept secret that he enjoyed peeking through curtains as much as his retired neighbor. A very early observation made by the Palm was how the whole street pulsated with constant activity. An early morning rooster faithfully announced the day's beginning.

The man across the street washed his perpetually parked RV every Saturday while playing *ranchera* music to serenade the whole block. Around noon the robust woman jingled her arrival as she pushed a cart full of ice cream bars in flavors called *Jamaica*, *Tamarindo*, and *Horchata*. Odds were if you looked up you'd see a ball whizzing through the air and into the arms of one of a dozen tanned-skin boys who scattered like ants when a car had to pass. Even at night while the houses slept, packs of dogs could be found strutting down the road like a leather-wearing gang of misfits.

The Palm grew quite comfortably in its new home. By the time it was seven feet tall, four summers had passed, and the family welcomed a baby girl. "*Felicidades*", Nacho exclaimed when the tidy bundle in hand-knitted blanket was introduced to him. Everyone was delighted by the arrival of the baby girl, including the

Palm. Mother and daughter made it a habit to sit on a blanket underneath its long, slender leaves. And the Palm cherished when it could play host to its guests - making them comfortable and sharing the very best it had to offer. During football seasons, the three of them listened to the brass and bass of the high school marching band as they practiced for their half-time shows right across the street. Years later even, mother, daughter, and Palm would play who-could-spot-the-two-boys-first while they ran laps during P.E.

While the boys walked to high school every morning, their little sister got dropped off a few blocks away at the diminutive catholic school dwelling tucked behind the church. Now, the Palm didn't know much about being catholic, but it did know that it shook with excitement every April when the little girl supervised her father as he cut off six to ten of its evergreen leaves, reminding him to, "be gentle, Dad, it's a living thing with feelings." He would then create a dozen or so small crosses out of the leaves to be blessed by Father Joe on Palm Sunday and dispersed to various locations for optimum blessings- above your bed as you slept, the dashboard of your car as you drove, and the front door for whatever else might come. The Palm never saw any other tree or bush get its leaves cut for the family so it knew there was something very powerful, if not magical, inside of it.

No amount of magic, however, could help Nacho the day he fell to one knee while tending to his old friend. It could only watch, completely helpless, as the old man struggled to breathe. A screaming ambulance took him away, and the Palm never saw Nacho again. It struggled to understand what it was feeling. Summer had come around again, but the Palm had no desire to drink or bask in the sun's warmth. July 4th always brought with it a booming thunder and light show, courtesy of the neighborhood kids who got their hands on (allegedly) illegal fireworks. Normally, the Palm looked forward to this night when the family would sit in lawn chairs beside it and gaze up at the brilliant explosions of red, green, blue and white light. This time was different. Something landed softly on the girl's shoulder. She turned to find a faded and frail leaf that had fallen from high above and noticed for the first time the drooping palms. She nagged her father to do something, but the regular watering made no difference in its appearance. After a couple of months, he admitted to his daughter that the sad tree might have to go.

On a cool Sunday afternoon the Palm (looking down at the dull cement sidewalk) caught sight of an approaching shadow. The Palm was confused and thought it had traveled back in time. The family had hired a new gardener, Enrique (who liked to be called *Quique*). He was Nacho's youngest son. Same eyes, nose, mouth, and as it would soon discover, as gentle hands as his father's. A few visits in, it became clear to the Palm that *Quique* missed Nacho immeasurably, but somehow found comfort in the company of the ailing tree. Something about running his hands through the same soft dirt his father's hands had nurtured chipped away at his grief. He remembered out loud the times he planted vegetables with his father in their own small backyard. And recounted the numerous lessons Nacho had taught him on planting, gardening, creating new life...and girls. "It's all the same, *mijo*" Nacho would say. That made the Palm laugh. It wasn't much longer before its leaves brightened and roots strengthened.

When it was time for the girl to leave for college, the boys had already moved out, the mother and father played with their first grandchild, and the cotton-candy-blue Chevy Malibu was little more than a dream. "Nothing stays the same" thought the Palm. The screen-door clinked shut and the Palm watched the mother coming straight towards it with her grandbaby in one arm and a blanket in the other.

La Estrella – The Star

    The sun had gone down by the time we reached San Diego County. On our right, we passed the twin water-power structures that unofficially mark the entrance to San Diego. We couldn't see the ocean, but knowing it was out there in the night made this part of the trip ominous, like we were traveling along the edge of the world. At least it would have if any of us was actually paying attention. But we weren't. If we had run out of gas, our incessant chatter could have fueled the car. Our high-pitched laughter was outdone only by the blaring music straining the twelve-year old speakers. Let's see, it would have been stuff like the Smiths, Depeche Mode, some Usher and Next, and a little bit of Tupac - it was 1998 after all, and we were L.A. girls.

    Irene had borrowed her mom's four-door Honda so we could take this road trip to El Valle de Guadalupe (a town outside of Ensenada, Mexico) where her grandparents' ranch was located. All of us had graduated high school two years earlier and scattered ourselves at colleges throughout the country. America was at Fresno State, Nadia at Yale, Irene and Martha at Wellesley, and I was at Berkeley. Our college lives had not completely taken over yet. The bond we shared as Garfield Bulldogs was still fed by cute handwritten letters in the mail, late night phone calls, and get-togethers during holidays and vacations.

It was probably around 10pm when we arrived at the ranch. Irene's grandparents were glad to have us, full of welcoming smiles as they led us to two large beds in a room full of mix-matched furniture and more than one *Virgen de Guadalupe* wall calendar. There was a relatively new but hardly ever used toilet installed. It may not have worked properly because I don't recall anyone attempting to use it. The elderly couple was accustomed to their double-seater outhouse we were inevitably acquainted with. America woke in the middle of the night to find her legs ravaged by starved mosquitoes- we wondered how she was the only one to get bitten and the only one who wore pants tucked into her socks to prevent it. She had to go to the restroom and decided Martha should go with her in case of snakes or wild dogs or, I don't know, *El Cucoy*. As it was told by America herself, they sat together damn near elbow-to-elbow in the double-seater outhouse - doing their business- and forever cementing the "America/Martha Bonding Experience" in our minds.

Their amplified giggles brought the rest of us out to a warm night underneath a perfectly starry sky. You just don't see that sort of thing in L.A. I thought I saw a bright star above my house once. Turned out to be a hovering plane. Entranced by the sheer multitude, we laid ourselves down on the grass and took in the sky. It reminded me of an old Lite-Brite I used to have - all those glowing little pegs stuck onto a black background. I remember thinking *this is a moment*. One of those moments you'll look back on and wish you could live again and again. But to say it out loud would somehow diminish its value. Maybe somewhere inside, I knew these moments we shared would become fewer. As time goes by, we'd most likely see less of each other.. But that sky didn't believe in time or "most likely". That sky was unequivocal and forever.

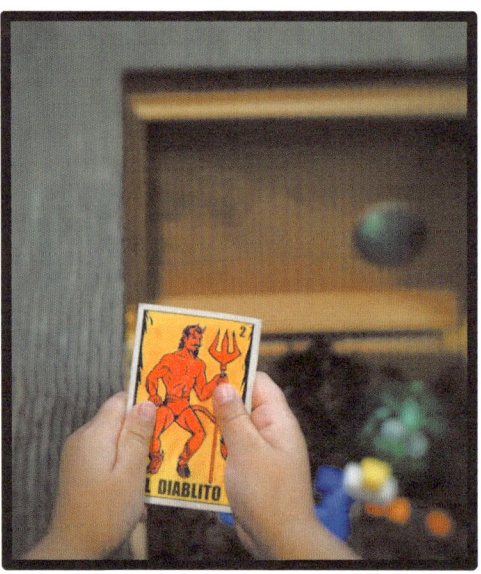

El Diablito – The Little Devil

Angel Baby

A Special Report on Good Boys Gone Bad.

Benicio was a good boy. By all rational accounts, he was known to display behavior modeling respect, obedience, and all around good-natured-ness. Born on a warm morning in June of 2011, he found his birth and the bright new world around him to be rather agreeable. Benicio's parents, a loving and nurturing couple who enforced peace and harmony in the home (it should be noted) often found him entertaining himself with toys and books. Not likely to throw unnecessary tantrums, he comfortably drifted from boisterous family gatherings to quiet alone time without much fuss. He knew without a doubt that Mami and Papi would be ready at any moment to adore his evolving charm or comfort his sorrows. Even at his most rambunctious moments, he remained sweet and, well, irresistible. It is not an exaggeration to point out that those closest to Benicio believed they had been truly blessed with an angel.

The change didn't occur overnight. A defining moment, however, can be pin-pointed to yet another warm morning in July of 2013 - the day he met his younger brother. Santiago was no more than 9 or 10 hours old, helpless in his mother's arms, but a threat nonetheless to Benicio's peaceful and harmonious world. He knew it the evening before when he was left alone with his grandparents for the night with neither an explanation nor apology. Aware of the potential issues of jealousy, Benicio's parents (it should be noted) made every attempt to express equal affection and show equal attention to both boys without exception. But, as you may well know, the immediate needs of an infant often outweigh those of a two-year-old even when you have the purest of intentions. This made Benicio angry. So angry he cried. He screamed. He kicked. Sometimes he went limp like a protester being dragged out of a government building - it just depended on the situation.

Then, one seemingly ordinary day, during an evening like any other, Benicio discovered something extraordinary. When he laughed, clapped his hands, or showed any signs of encouragement toward Santiago's shenanigans, by golly, he would do it again! Even if it was naughty. Even if his parents didn't like it. Holy smokes! The kid would do anything for his big brother. Now, a nice boy, an angel if you will, would take this newfound knowledge and encourage his little brother to do good, helpful things - like, oh I don't know, gently place the metal toy truck in the toy box instead of flinging it at the 50 inch flat screen. Or grab a coloring book from the bottom shelf and not doodle a Crayola trail from one end of the hallway to the other. Better yet, simply eat the bowl of spaghetti rather than scatter tomato sauce and sticky angel hair across the kitchen floor...Do you know how tricky that is to clean up? But Benicio, with the sweet smile, was no angel.

Oh, a whole new world had opened up for Benicio. Like the little red, horned figure on the shoulder of Santiago, he had the power to make him do unspeakable things. With a twinkle in his eye and the slightest grin, he got his little brother to spit orange juice on the kitchen floor which, despite the cleaning efforts of their parents, still attracted a parade of presumptuous ants the next morning. While playing outside Santiago was quite content with kicking around the multitude of rocks, but Benicio wasn't. In a fit of giggles, he suggested that his little brother throw them in the pool - who cared that it had painstakingly been cleaned the day before by Papi himself? You bet your bottom dollar they all ended up in the pool! And then there was the time Benicio encouraged his little brother to sprinkle handfuls of sand onto his head, "It's fun, Santi, go ahead, do it." When Mami called them to get inside the house, they ran directly to Mami and Papi's bed, and left a sandy surprise for Mami and Papi when they got into bed that night. Mami and Papi emptied the sandbox the next day.

In a recent interview with the boys' parents they admit they are at a loss for any concrete explanation as to Benicio's change in behavior but it could have something to do with the water. And, for those of you interested in where they stand currently, well, they had these words to share:
"The boys have teamed up. They equally influence each other. It is our cross to bear."

El Valiente – The Brave One

Back in 2000, I started recording family ghost stories as told to me by my mom, my grandma, and letters from my Aunt Socorro. Around that time, I was taking an English course on memoirs, and, for an assignment, I presented those family ghost stories as if they were being told to me and my other cousins by our Uncle George. Why did I choose my Uncle George as the storyteller? Because I (and my cousins who were present) share a vivid memory of one night when we were all at his house, in my cousin Lorrie's room, waiting for him to tell us a ghost story. I can't remember what his story was about (something about an old outhouse) but the anticipation and excitement are what fuels this memory. That and the 10 feet leap into Uncle George's lap that cousin Desiree took when Ruben pounded on the window from the backyard right at the climactic moment! Here is the introduction to that memoir assignment exactly as I wrote it, almost.

*****

The girls piled themselves onto the cushy queen-sized bed, wrapped up in patterned quilts and watched a single candle flicker its subtle glow upon the shadowed walls. They chattered and chuckled with excitement as they awaited their Uncle George's entrance. What a fantastic figure of power Uncle George was - in the eyes and perspectives of these girls! He was a stout, block-shaped man who spoke with a booming crash of a voice that shook walls and woke sleeping spirits. He had slicked-back black hair and a full mustache that curled down around the corners of his mouth. Just underneath the short sleeves of his ironed white t-shirts, the girls could see the green shading of old tattoos on his veined arms. They were the first punctuation to his intimidating image. Even for all his dark and threatening physical attributes, Uncle George was a gentle man - gentle with children, that is. The moment he entered the room where the girls anxiously awaited him, they were overcome with the strength of his protection. As far as they knew, no person, ghost or goblin would dare to cross his path. Feeling the warm security of each other on the queen-size bed and the presence of their uncle, sitting on a chair beside them, they eagerly relaxed into position to hear the wonders and mysteries of their family ghost stories.

And that's how I'll always remember my Uncle George.

El Corazon – The Heart

    I don't recall the first time we met - what was said or what I was thinking - but I can see you vividly in my memory, strutting through the lobby with that basketball player hop to your step and a bright toothy smile that practically leaped out to shake my hand. You ask me now for the one moment when I knew I loved you. I reply with, "I don't know."

    You: What do you mean you don't know?

    Me: It's impossible to pinpoint.

    You: Try.

    Me: (deep sigh) Sometime during that first smile. After the initial cconfidence of all those teeth eased into *who is she* curiosity.

    Tucked inside of your offer to pick me up after my late class so I wouldn't be on the bus alone, then on the side streets you'd take to spend more time with me.

    Wrapped up in those days I looked forward to working next to you and those other days that melted away without you.

Buried deep in our first kiss, like our feet in the cold sand; an October sunset over the beach. Cute, you're ticklish on your ear. I discovered that right away.

Hiding in the bathroom that time I didn't want to *go* in front of you. You said, "It's me and you now, right? If there ever comes a day you can't do things for yourself, I'll be the one to take care of you."

Enveloped in your words, "Stay there. I'm coming to get you" because I found out my grandma had passed, and I was crying all alone.

Shrouded in the revelation that you were everything I hadn't been looking for because I didn't know you could exist.

You: (cocking your head to the side) I said the *one* moment you knew you loved me.

Me: (a whisper) We *are* that moment.

CPSIA information can be obtained at www.ICGtesting.com
Printed in the USA
BVIW12n1640200817
492509BV00001B/1